Ghostyshocks and the Three Scares

Written by Laurence Anholt
Illustrated by Arthur Robins

Reader beware! You're in for a *bear*.
(Well, three bears actually.)

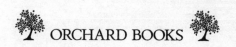
ORCHARD BOOKS

It was a dark and stormy night. Three bears were moving into an old house in a spooky forest.

Their terrible howls echoed through the trees and terrified the people of the nearby village.

There was a huge hairy Daddy Bear howl:
"WOOO-HOOOOO!"

A middle-sized Mummy Bear howl:
"Yoo-hoo!"

And a terrible
teeny-weeny Baby
Bear howl: "Wheee!"

7

The more the villagers heard, the more nervous they became. A story went around that their new neighbours were VAMPIRE BEARS!

The people of the village refused to go near the forest, and visitors would find them pale and trembling.

There was one girl who was more afraid than anyone. The slightest squeak made her jump. Even the tiniest spider made her SCREAM!

When anyone asked her name, she would reply:

It's G-G-G...

Glenda Gobstopper?

NO. G-G-G...

Good King Wenceslas?

No. G-G-G...

Two things frightened Ghostyshocks
more than anything else in the world. The
first was the dark, dangerous forest, and
the second was...VAMPIRE BEARS!!!

Now, Ghostyshocks lived with her old granny, and they were terribly poor. Granny often suggested that Ghostyshocks should try to earn some money, but Ghostyshocks was far too nervous to get a job.

"Couldn't you do a little baby-sitting, dear?" her granny would ask.

But G-Granny, I might meet the three b-b-b...

Three baby baboons, dear?

No. Three b-b-b...

Three blind mice, dear?

NO. The THREE B-B-BEARS!

One foggy winter's day, Ghostyshocks's granny was in bed with a bad cold.

"Ghostyshocks, the fire has gone out," she said. "You must go out to collect more wood."

Ghostyshocks went pale. There was only one place to collect wood...

"I'm sorry, Ghostyshocks," said her granny, "But you're a big girl now, and the house is cold."

And so it was that Ghostyshocks crept
outside, trembling from top to toe.

She climbed the little path from the
village, and entered the creepy black forest.

At that very moment, the three bears were waking up.

Daddy Bear yawned a huge daddy-sized yawn: "WOOO-HOOOOO!"

Mummy Bear yawned a middle-sized yawn:
"Yoo-hoo!"

And teeny-weeny Baby Bear yawned a
teeny-weeny baby-sized yawn: "Wheee!"

Down in the village, every door and window banged shut.

Deep in the forest, poor Ghostyshocks huddled beneath a blueberry bush.

In their new house, the three bears got dressed and went downstairs.

Mummy Bear poured out their breakfast. It looked delicious – bright red and steaming!

A big red bowlful for Daddy Bear. A middle-sized red bowlful for Mummy Bear. And a teeny-weeny red bowlful for Baby Bear.

23

But – oh dear! – their breakfast was far too hot.

Daddy Bear burnt his tongue, and howled a HUGE Daddy Bear howl: "WOOO-HOOOOO!"

Mummy Bear burnt her tongue, and howled a middle-sized howl: "Yoo-hoo!"

And teeny-weeny Baby Bear burnt
his tongue, and howled a teeny-weeny
baby-sized howl: "Wheee!"

Down in the village, everyone crawled under their tables and beds, and hugged each other in fear.

Deep, deep in the darkest part of the dark
and dangerous forest, Ghostyshocks was as
jittery as a jellyfish.

She ran off the path and hid in the
undergrowth.

"Why are you out all alone?" asked a deer.

At the bears' house, Daddy Bear said, "*Oooh*, this breakfast is far too hot, Mummy Bear. I'll tell you what, let's have a nice walk while it cools off. Come on, Baby Bear, grab your wellies."

So the three bears put on their boots, and went out into the forest for a stroll.

By now, Ghostyshocks had wandered further and further from the path. Twigs scratched at her face like wicked witches' fingers. To her horror, she realised that she was completely lost.

So Ghostyshocks stumbled up to the huge black door, and with a shaky finger rang the bell. No one answered, but the door slowly creaked open. *CRE-E-EAK!*

Ghostyshocks stepped inside. Her stomach felt knotted like knitted knickers, and her knees were knocking nervously.

Before her was a large table. Three places were set for breakfast. There was a big bowl, a middle-sized bowl, and a teeny-weeny baby bowl.

But what was *inside* the bowls?

Ghostyshocks dipped
her finger into the big bowl.
"*Uuurgh!*" she gasped.
"It's d-d-disgusting!"

She dipped a finger into
the middle-sized bowl.
"W-w-what *is* it?"

She picked up
the teeny-weeny
baby bowl, and stared
at the red liquid inside.

She remembered the terrible stories of
vampire bears, and suddenly she shrieked,
"It must be BL-BL-BLOOD!!!"

Ghostyshocks was shaking so much that she spilt the whole bowl all down her clean dress.

"EEEEEEEEEKK!" she screamed.

She had to sit down before she fainted with fright.

She found a huge chair, but it was far too big.

She found a middle-sized chair, but that was too hard.

She found a teeny-weeny baby-sized high-chair and that was too small, but she sat in it anyway.

CR-R-R-RA-A-A-ACK!

The teeny-weeny high-chair shattered into teeny-tiny pieces.

"Aaargh!" screamed Ghostyshocks, and
she ran out and up the twisting staircase.

Gasping for breath, she stumbled into a bedroom. Then, to her horror, Ghostyshocks heard voices downstairs:

"HOI! Somebody's been poking their paws in my breakfast!" roared a huge, great voice.

"And somebody's been playing with my breakfast. How unhygienic," said a middle-sized voice.

"And somebody's been mucking about with my breakfast," said a teeny-weeny voice, "and spilt the whole bowl."

Ghostyshocks searched desperately for a place to hide. She pulled back the covers on a huge bed, but they'd easily spot her in there.

She tried to hide in the middle-sized bed, but the bears would look there too.

Then Ghostyshocks noticed a teeny-weeny bed, in the far corner of the room. She crawled inside and pulled the sheets right over her head.

"Hoi! Somebody's been sitting in my chair!" roared a huge, great voice downstairs.

"And somebody's been sitting in my chair," said a middle-sized voice.

"And somebody's been sitting in my chair," said a teeny-weeny voice, "and they've smashed it into teeny-tiny pieces."

Ghostyshocks heard footsteps creaking up the stairs, and coming slowly along the dark corridor.

They came closer...

and closer...

and *closer!*

The door was slowly pushed open...

"Somebody's been lying in my bed!" roared a huge, great voice.

"And somebody's been lying in my bed," said a middle-sized voice.

Ghostyshocks closed her eyes as tight as she could, and lay frozen with fear. She heard the loud breathing of the bears as they searched the room. Closer...and closer...and *closer!*

Suddenly, a hairy paw grabbed the blankets on the teeny-weeny bed, and tore them away.

The three bears stared at Ghostyshocks. She was as white as a sheet and covered with a ghastly red stain.

"Somebody's been bumped-off in my bed," squeaked a teeny-weeny voice, "and *she's still there!*"

"WOOO-HOOOOO!" screamed the big Daddy Bear.

"Yoo-hoo!" yelled the middle-sized Mummy Bear.

"Wheee!" squealed the teeny-weeny Baby Bear.

The three bears were terrified. They turned and ran for the door.

"W-w-wait," said Ghostyshocks, sitting up in bed.

"Promise you won't hurt me," said the
teeny-weeny Baby Bear.

"Of c-c-course I won't," said Ghostyshocks.

"Well, let's all go downstairs and have some breakfast," said Mummy Bear. "I've made some lovely tomato soup, and I'm sure it's cool now."

"Tomato soup?" said Ghostyshocks. "Does that mean you're not v-v-v...? I thought you were v-v-v...?"

"Vegetarians, dear? Of course we are.
Daddy Bear grows all our own vegetables."

So the three bears and Ghostyshocks had breakfast together.

58

Mummy Bear washed Ghostyshocks's dress, and Daddy Bear said it didn't matter at all about the teeny-weeny high-chair because Baby Bear was getting quite big now. He put all the pieces of wood into Ghostyshocks's bag for firewood.

"We must come down and meet your granny and everyone in the village," said Mummy Bear. "We wanted to visit, only we don't like leaving little Baby Bear."

"I'm the best baby-sitter for miles around," said Ghostyshocks. "Three pounds an hour. Four pounds at weekends. You provide tea, coffee and snacks...and easy on the tomato soup."

61

"But wouldn't you be nervous, out here with just Baby Bear?" asked Daddy Bear.

"Who me?" said Ghostyshocks, "Nothing scares me. We'll play in the forest, and tell each other ghost stories…"

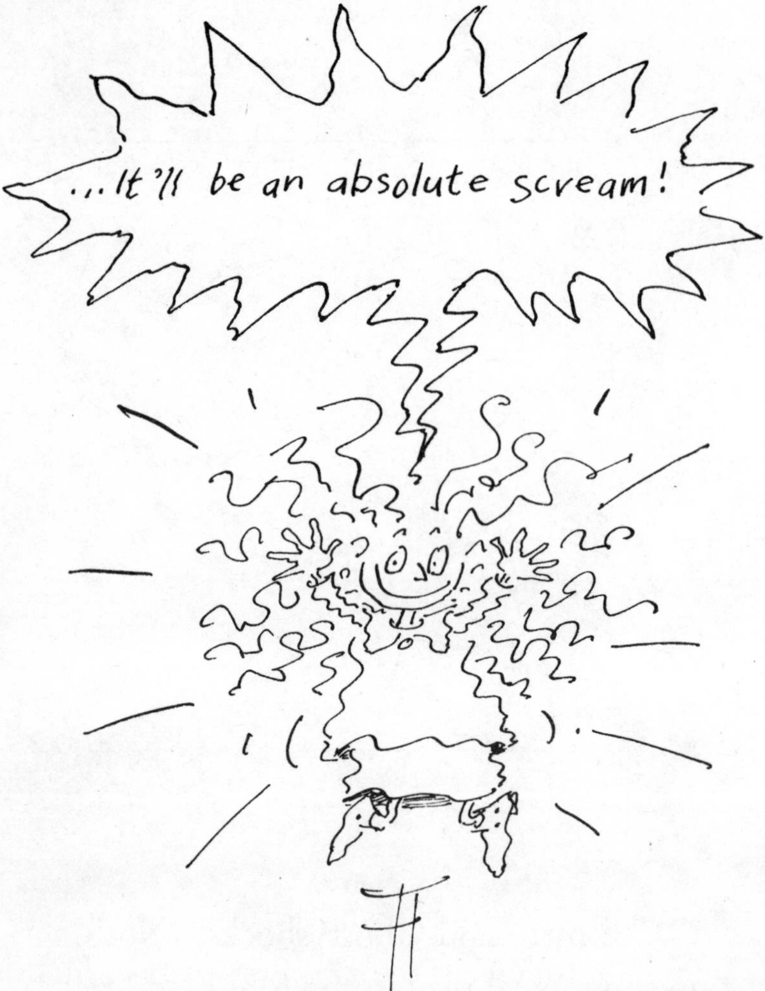
...It'll be an absolute scream!